I'm Special Because . . .

Kevin Pearce

NEIGHBORHOOD READERS

Rosen Classroom Books & Materials™

New York

"Carmen, do you know why you are special?" said Mom.
"Yes, I do!" said Carmen.

"I am special because I can hop on one foot!" said Carmen. "I like to hop!"

“I am special because I like to laugh!”
said Carmen.
“I laugh a lot!”

"I am special because I like to read books!" said Carmen. "Books are fun to read!"

“I am special because I look after my brother!” said Carmen. “I love my brother!”

"I am special because I am a good friend!" said Carmen. "I like to share!"

"Yes!" said Mom.
"You are special because there is no one like you!"